A SWINGIN' YULE

10 JAZZY CHRISTMAS SONGS

CD INCLUDED

Arranged for Int.-Adv. Piano
by Steve Calderone
with play-along CD

Project Manager: Tony Esposito
Art Layout: Ken Rehm

AN INTRODUCTION

Among the countless collections of Christmas piano arrangements, which have been available for years, **A SWINGIN' YULE** is indeed unique. In this collection, the traditional favorites have been adapted with extensive use of jazz harmonies and an uplifting swing feel. These settings are unconventional, including the playfully rhythmic as well as the peacefully serene. But they are all fun to play and will fit into any evening performance from the grand ballroom to the living room—sure to enhance every Christmas celebration.

A SHORT BIO

For more than twenty years, **Steve Calderone** has been teaching, arranging, and playing for theater groups, folk groups, and individual students. He is versatile and eclectic, feeling at home performing on the concert stage or leading a coffeehouse sing-along. He studied music at the College of the Holy Cross in Worcester, Massachusetts, where he once performed *Rhapsody in Blue* with orchestra and then led the cast and orchestra as musical director of a theatrical production of *Pippin,* all during the same week. He has played for or directed more than a dozen church music groups and more than two dozen theatrical productions. His piano students have ranged in age from five to 75. He also toured Europe with a vocal and instrumental group in 1976, and since the 1980s, he has played during many appearances on the local televised program, "Chalice of Salvation." During every December, he can be found leading the holiday merriment at several Christmas season celebrations. Here is your chance to share in that musical enjoyment.

This collection is dedicated to my parents Connie and Joe, my wife Marie, and our daughter Elizabeth.

CONTENTS

TRACKING SHEET*

*The CD included in this book has been recorded in stereo so that the music for each hand can be practiced individually by sliding the balance to one side or the other. Also, clicks have been added to each song to help you find the starting point as well as set up the rhythm and tempo. Good luck and enjoy!

JOY TO THE WORLD

Words by
ISAAC WATTS

Music by GEORGE F. HANDEL
Arranged by STEVE CALDERONE

Moving along ♩ = 176

RINGING SINGING CHRISTMAS

Carol of the Bells
Sing We Now of Christmas

UKRAINIAN CAROL
FRENCH CAROL
Arranged by STEVE CALDERONE

THE HOLLY AND THE IVY

TRADITIONAL ENGLISH
Arranged by STEVE CALDERONE

The Holly and the Ivy - 5 - 1
AF9928CD

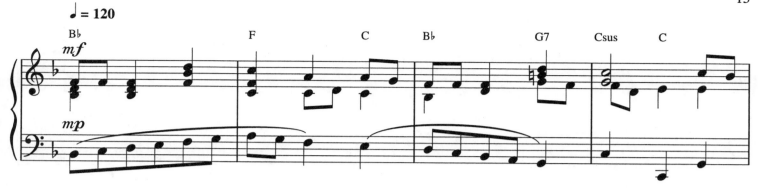

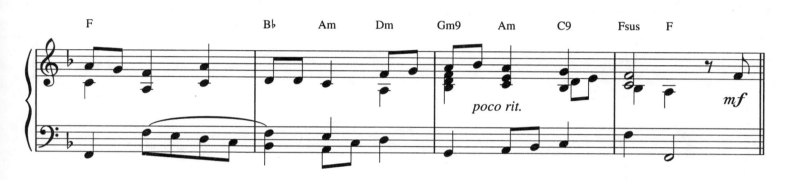

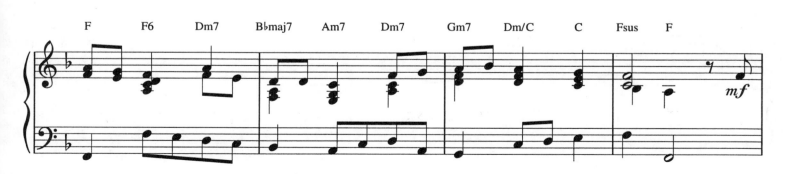

The Holly and the Ivy - 5 - 3
AF9928CD

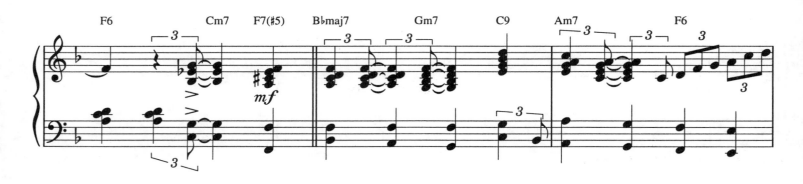

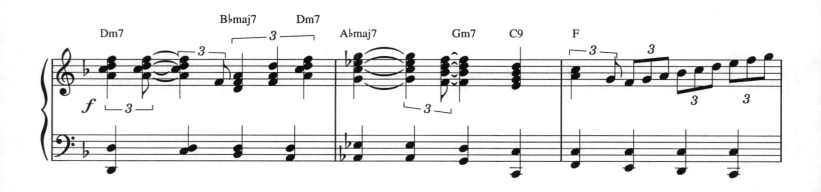

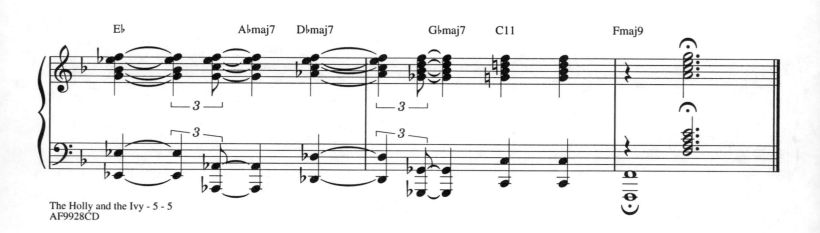

COVENTRY KINGS

We Three Kings of Orient Are
The Coventry Carol

Words and Music by
Rev. JOHN HENRY HOPKINS

TRADITIONAL ENGLISH CAROL
Arranged by STEVE CALDERONE

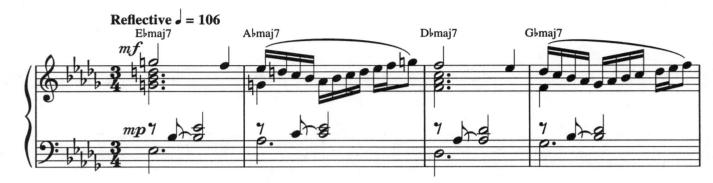

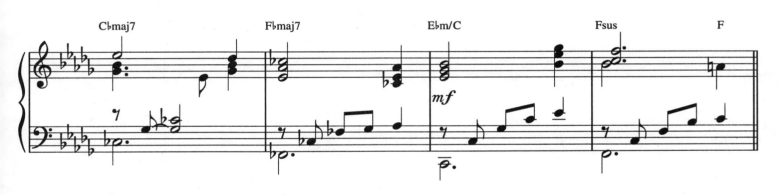

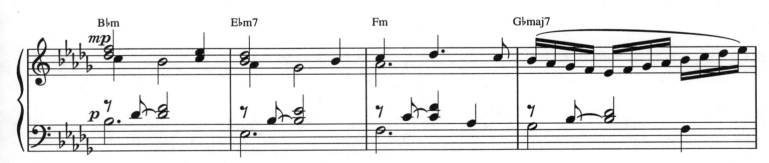

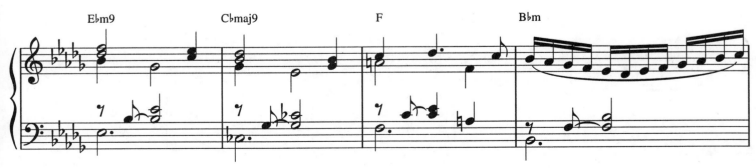

Coventry Kings - 8 - 1
AF9928CD

IT CAME UPON THE MIDNIGHT CLEAR

Words by
EDMUND H. SEARS

Music by
RICHARD S. WILLIS
Arranged by STEVE CALDERONE

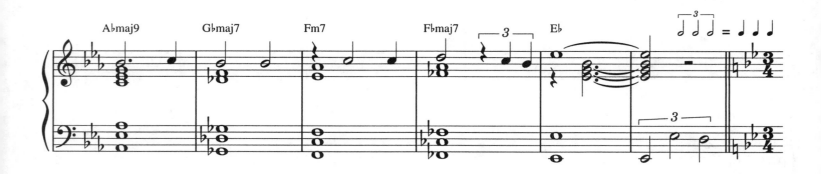

It Came Upon the Midnight Clear - 5 - 4
AF9928CD

It Came Upon the Midnight Clear - 5 - 5
AF9928CD

GOOD CHRISTIAN MEN, REJOICE

Words by
JOHN MASON NEALE

(In Dulci Jubilo)
OLD GERMAN SONG
Arranged by STEVE CALDERONE

Good Christian Men, Rejoice - 4 - 1
AF9928CD

34

ANGEL SOUNDS

Hark! The Herald Angels Sing
Angels We Have Heard On High

Words by CHARLES WESLEY
Music by FELIX MENDELSSOHN

TRADITIONAL
WESTMINSTER CAROL
Arranged by STEVE CALDERONE

Angel Sounds - 5 - 1
AF9928CD

O HOLY NIGHT
(Cantique de Noel)

Words by
JOHN S. DWIGHT

Music by
ADOLPHE CHARLES ADAM
Arranged by STEVE CALDERONE

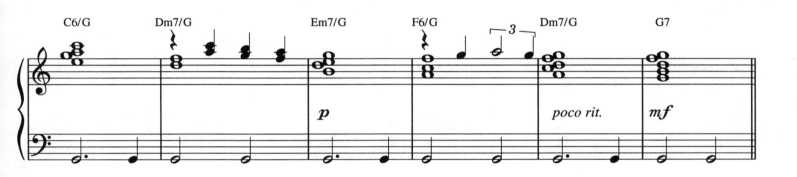

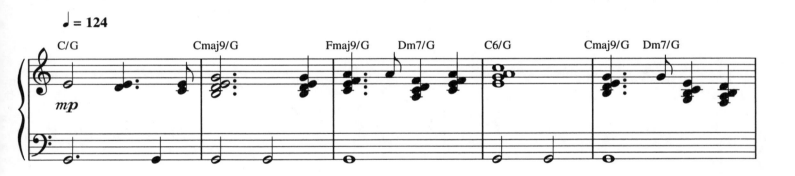

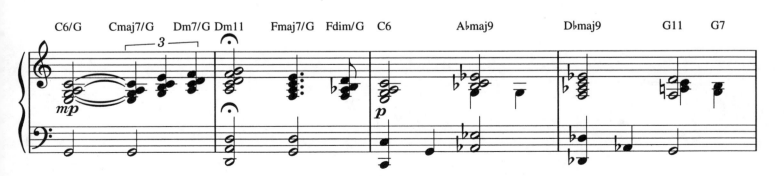

O Holy Night - 3 - 1
AF9928CD

42

O Holy Night - 3 - 2
AF9928CD

O Holy Night - 3 - 3
AF9928CD

A JOLLY JINGLE

Jolly Old St. Nicholas
Jingle Bells

TRADITIONAL
Words and Music by
JAMES PIERPONT
Arranged by STEVE CALDERONE

A Jolly Jingle - 6 - 1
AF9928CD

A Jolly Jingle - 6 - 4
AF9928CD

48

A Jolly Jingle - 6 - 6
AF9928CD

SILENT NOEL

A Diatonic Duet with
The First Noel and Silent Night

Silent Night
Music by FRANZ GRUBER
Words by JOSEPH MOHR

The First Noel
TRADITIONAL ENGLISH CAROL
Arranged by STEVE CALDERONE

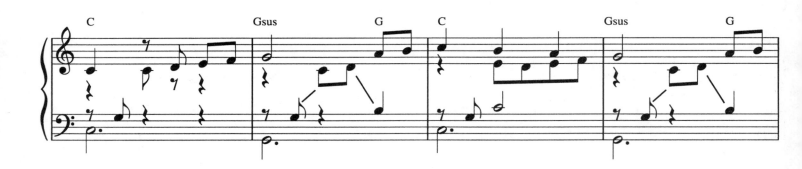

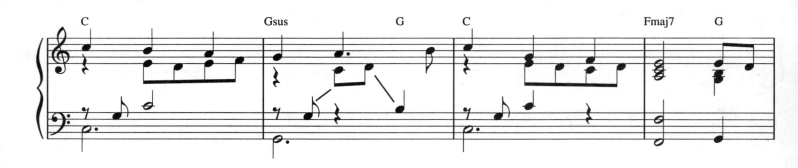

A Silent Noel - 6 - 1
AF9928CD

A Silent Noel - 6 - 4
AF9928CD

A Swingin' Yule